Cambridge English Readers

Level 4

Series editor: Philip Prowse

Berlin Express

Michael Austen

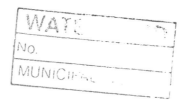

CAMBRIDGE
UNIVERSITY PRESS

CAMBRIDGE UNIVERSITY PRESS

Cambridge, New York, Melbourne, Madrid, Cape Town, Singapore,
São Paulo, Delhi, Dubai, Tokyo

Cambridge University Press
The Edinburgh Building, Cambridge CB2 8RU, UK

www.cambridge.org
Information on this title: www.cambridge.org/9780521174909

First published 2010

Michael Austen has asserted his right to be identified as the Author of the Work in
accordance with the Copyright, Designs and Patents Act 1988.

Printed in China by Sheck Wah Tong Printing Press Limited
Typeset by Aptara Inc.
Map artwork by Malcolm Barnes

A catalogue record for this publication is available from the British Library.

ISBN 978-0-521-17490-9 paperback
ISBN 978-0-521-17511-1 paperback plus audio CD pack

Contents

Characters

Hiro Adachi: a Japanese university student, studying in England.
Akiko: Hiro's ex-girlfriend
The Shark / Erik Björnson: an old man Hiro meets on the train
Karl Meier: a German man in Berlin
Franz Schubert: a bodyguard

Places in the story

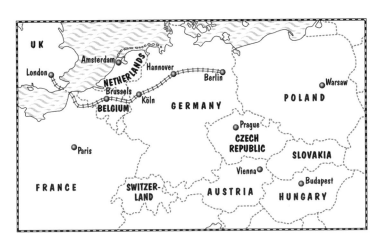

Chapter 1   *The past and the future*

The train was really flying along now. The buildings, fields and trees all seemed to race by. A bridge shot past the window. Then a station. Hiro put his face nearer the glass to see the name, but they were travelling so fast it was impossible to read. Hiro wondered if they were travelling faster than the *Shinkansen*, the world-famous Bullet Train of Japan. He looked up at the small screen above the door, which showed the speed – 294 kilometres per hour! He watched the numbers as they slowly increased. 296 … 298 … All of a sudden, they were there: 301 kph! Well, that was something exciting to tell …

And then it hit him all over again. Yes, but who would he tell? If it had been a month ago – even two weeks – he would have sent Akiko a text. But since their break-up she didn't want to hear from him. 'Don't send me any messages, because I won't reply,' she had told him angrily. 'If you'd rather have a photo of Yuki than me on your phone, that's fine. Just don't expect me to be your girlfriend any more!'

Hiro looked sadly out of the window again. Where were they? He knew they'd left Belgium and were in Germany now because he'd seen a sign just before the last station. But what city came next? Was it Köln? In Köln, Hiro had to change trains. He wondered if he should ask the middle-aged woman sitting opposite. But just when he had decided not to, the train flew past a village and the woman suddenly spoke to him in English.

'Ha!' she said. 'There's my village! I'll be home in an hour. It's only ten minutes to Köln!'

Hiro smiled politely. The woman was a little bossy-looking and never seemed to sit still.

'But *you* are a long way from home ...' she went on. 'Are you Japanese?'

Hiro nodded. He didn't feel much like chatting, but it was clear the woman did. 'Yes,' he said, 'but I'm studying in England. I'm on a Study Year Abroad programme. This is my summer holiday.'

'Very good! And where are you going?' she went on.

'Berlin. I have an InterRail ticket,' Hiro answered, then seeing the confused look on her face, guessed he'd better explain. 'That means I can use my ticket to travel anywhere in Europe. Berlin is my first stop.'

'How exciting! But you're travelling alone. That's very brave.'

Hiro paused. 'My friends ...' he began. 'My friends ... couldn't come.'

'Oh, that's too bad,' the woman answered. She was about to say something else when her mobile phone rang. She searched excitedly in her bag, then began a loud conversation in German on her phone.

Hiro picked up his book. It was an American thriller – he'd brought it with him to practise his English – and with two violent murders already it was quite exciting. But Hiro couldn't read now. He thought sadly about what he'd just told the woman. It wasn't really the truth. The truth was that he and Akiko had planned to have a holiday together, but after their argument everything had changed. They'd been so happy all the time they'd been together. She was on the same course in England and they'd met in the first week. And they'd never argued at all. So, then to get jealous about a dog! That was just crazy!

Hiro reached into his pocket and took out his own mobile phone. With one easy movement, he opened it and watched the screen come to life. For a moment or two he looked at his screensaver – the picture that appeared when he turned on his phone. It was a photo of Yuki, his beautiful twelve-year-old golden retriever, the most wonderful dog in the world. Then he chose 'My photos' from the menu on the side of the screen. Almost immediately, a picture of Akiko appeared. It was his favourite photo of her – the one at the restaurant where he'd taken her for her birthday. She looked so happy and so pretty! Hiro shook his head and quickly went back to the picture of the dog.

The argument had come out of nowhere. They'd been planning a beach holiday in southern Spain. When he'd invited his friends Ayumu and Daijiro and their girlfriends, Akiko had seemed happy enough. But then something had changed. He said he wished they could take Yuki as well, and all of sudden Akiko had got angry. After that everything Hiro said seemed to make her angrier. She'd started talking about his screensaver, and the next thing he knew she was shouting that she didn't want to see him ever again. It was just unbelievable. One moment he had a girlfriend, the next he didn't. Now, apparently, she'd gone off to Scotland with a couple of her friends. But he wasn't even sure of that. Their eight-month relationship had just exploded like a bomb.

All of a sudden Hiro realised a tear was running down his cheek. Angrily, he brushed it away. The woman opposite was still talking loudly into her phone, so she hadn't seen the tear. But this was no way for a twenty-year-old Japanese man to behave. Hurriedly, he got out his InterRail map and pretended to study it closely. He'd left London that morning very early and taken the Eurostar to Brussels in Belgium. From there he'd caught this train going to Köln, and in Köln he would get the train to Berlin. But where would he go after that? Prague, the capital of the Czech Republic, was only five hours by train from Berlin. Then, he could go to Vienna, maybe. If there was time he might even get to Budapest. How many new countries would he visit this trip? If he went to all those cities, it would make five!

Hiro began to feel more cheerful. He sat up and looked out of the window again at the countryside flying past. It seemed different and new all of a sudden. 'Yes,' Hiro thought, 'I will have an exciting and adventurous holiday. I'm not going to be sad. From this moment, Akiko is part of history. No more looking back; I will only look forward from now on.'

Chapter 2   *A meeting with a shark*

The train raced on for five minutes more, then began to slow down. The woman closed her phone and busily collected her things together.

'So, Köln!' she said brightly and stood up. 'Now I must find my husband and you must go to the Berlin train. Platform 2.'

Soon the train came to a stop and Hiro followed the woman off on to the platform. Immediately after they'd said goodbye, she called loudly to a tired-looking man waiting at the bottom of a staircase. The man hurried over to her, then followed her up the stairs, carrying all her bags.

Hiro made his way to Platform 2. He had half an hour to wait for his next train and, for some reason, sitting on the station made him feel lonely again. As soon as the train arrived, he climbed in. He found an empty seat, then sat looking out at the crowd of people outside the window. Hiro noticed an attractive blonde girl with a big blue bag getting on the train. He wondered if the girl might come and sit in the seat opposite him. But after taking a few steps towards him, she chose a seat three rows away. Hiro was disappointed.

Then a man with silvery-grey hair, wearing a grey raincoat got on. He was pulling a small suitcase on wheels. Hiro watched him come closer. He stopped some way down the train and spoke to one of the people there, giving a wide toothy smile. Hiro didn't like the look of the man. There was something about his smile, his grey clothes and the silent way he moved, which reminded Hiro of a shark. The man came down the train towards him. Hiro hoped the man would walk past. But he didn't.

'Excuse me,' the man said in English, giving the same smile. 'Is anyone sitting here?'

Hiro had no choice. As well as the seat beside him, the two opposite were free. 'No,' he said, 'of course …'

'Thank you so much,' the man answered.

The man pushed his suitcase under the seat, then sat down opposite Hiro. Hiro felt uncomfortable. The man's eyes seemed very small and his teeth very sharp. Hiro was reminded of a shark once again. He imagined the man swimming towards him and smiling. The smile made Hiro feel very cold, as if an icy hand had touched the back of his neck. He watched as the man took off his grey raincoat, took a mobile phone from the coat pocket and put the phone on the table between them. Hiro noticed the man's hands. They looked terribly clean and the fingernails perfect. Hiro wondered if the man might be a dentist.

The train pulled out of the station. Hiro tried to look away from the man and read his book again, but something kept making him look up. The man had taken a newspaper from his case and put on a pair of glasses now. He looked quite strong, but with his grey hair, Hiro guessed he must be in his mid-sixties, even seventy perhaps. After a while, the man put down the newspaper and checked his phone. He did everything very carefully, holding the phone at a distance, and looking at the screen. His fingers moved lightly over the keys. After a couple of minutes, the man put the phone on to the table, sat back in his seat and closed his eyes. Hiro suddenly felt much calmer. The man had made him nervous. It was like being near a dangerous animal. 'Yes,' Hiro decided, 'he's not a man; he's a shark.'

Hiro relaxed and read his book. The train was soon racing along again and his book was very exciting. The next time he checked his watch it was after four o'clock. He looked at the man opposite. 'Good, the Shark is still sleeping,' he thought.

Hiro got out his guidebook and tried to decide what to do when he reached Berlin. He had booked a room in a cheap hotel, the Hotel Alma, in an area called Kreuzberg. But how would he get there? There seemed to be an underground train called the U-Bahn, but also an overground one, the S-Bahn. Which one should he use?

All of a sudden, the train braked sharply and a number of things happened at once. The braking was so hard that a woman walking down the train fell across the table between Hiro and the Shark. As she fell, she knocked the Shark's newspaper and phone off the table and on to the seat beside Hiro. At the same moment the Shark jumped up and his hand shot out. But instead of helping the woman, he reached out across the table to try to get his things back. Hiro was very surprised. The Shark couldn't reach his things but, after a moment, he became quite pleasant again. Speaking in German, he took the woman's arm and helped her up. A conversation followed, then the woman went away. The Shark sat down again. Almost immediately, he said,

'You have my mobile phone, I believe.'

Hiro didn't understand for a moment. Then he looked down at the seat beside him and saw the man's phone on his jacket. Hiro was surprised because he thought he'd put his own phone there. He picked up the phone and passed it across.

'I'm sorry,' he said.

'That's all right,' the Shark said, taking the phone. As he did so, their hands touched. The Shark's hand felt cold. 'These trains are so dangerous,' he went on. 'They are too fast! I am always nervous travelling in this country.'

'Yes,' Hiro answered.

'Will you excuse me for a moment?' the man said. 'Please be so kind to keep my seat for me.'

Without waiting for an answer, he picked up his phone and walked up the train to the toilet. Hiro watched the Shark close the toilet door, then saw the light above the door come on.

For a moment nothing happened, then Hiro heard the small ringing sound his phone made when a text message came through. He looked down. Under his jacket, he found his phone. So, it was there after all. His heart gave a tiny jump. Could it be a text from Akiko? He picked up the phone and pressed a key to open the message.

For a second or two he didn't understand. He could understand the English, but not what it meant. He read it twice.

MEET BRANDENBURG GATE 1 PM TOMORROW. COLLECT EQUIPMENT AND HALF FEE.

It was another two or three seconds before Hiro realised the phone wasn't his.

Chapter 3 *An amusing mistake*

Hiro stared at the phone. Of course, he understood what had happened now – the Shark's phone was a Nokia just like his. In his excitement to check the message, Hiro hadn't noticed there was no screensaver, no photo of his dog.

Well, it was a simple mistake and there was nothing to feel guilty about. When the Shark returned from the toilet, Hiro would hand back the phone and apologise. The message didn't seem that private. Hiro knew the Brandenburg Gate was one of the most famous sights in Berlin. So, the man was meeting someone there. He was going to collect some equipment and half his fee. Surely there wasn't anything very private about that?

Hiro put the phone down and looked up. He wondered if the Shark had checked Hiro's phone and discovered the mistake, too. The light was still on above the toilet door. Perhaps even at this moment the Shark was reading one of the love messages Akiko had sent Hiro before their break-up. Hiro had saved seven or eight of them.

Hiro read the message on the Shark's phone once more. Perhaps it was the result of the book he was reading with all its murders, but the more Hiro looked at the message, the more uncomfortable he felt. There seemed to be something odd about it, something that wasn't quite right. He paused for a second, then did something really stupid. He knew it was stupid even before he did it, but it was just so easy. He pressed the Inbox key on the Shark's phone, and found the message list. The first message on the list – the one he'd just read – was from someone called 'M'. Hiro picked the next message. It was also from 'M'. Hiro looked up once more. It was safe: the toilet light was still on. He opened the message. The little screen filled immediately.

BERLIN ASSIGNMENT HOTEL ADLON ROOM 319 TUESDAY AFTER 8PM. HALF FEE AT MEETING, HALF ON COMPLETION.

Hiro wasn't sure he understood. His heart was beating fast. Part of the message was obvious: tomorrow was Tuesday and the Hotel Adlon must be in Berlin. He knew what a fee was, too: money that is paid for doing something. But what about the rest? Wasn't 'assignment' another word for 'job'? The word sounded a little bit odd. Wasn't 'assignment' a word a writer would use in a thriller to mean …? No, that was a crazy thought! 'It must be the effect of that silly book I'm reading,' Hiro said to himself.

The next moment his heart stopped. When he looked up, the light above the toilet had gone out. Not only that, but the door was opening and the Shark was coming out. The old man was already making his way back towards him.

Hiro had to act fast. He closed the message, then dropped the phone back on to the seat beside him. Now he could relax: the Shark would never know Hiro had been reading the messages. Hiro watched the man come up.

A second later, Hiro realised his mistake. Of course the Shark would know! The last message had been received while he was in the toilet and Hiro had opened it then. It wouldn't show as a 'New Message' now, but as one that had been 'Read'. Hiro picked up the phone just as the Shark arrived.

Even before he sat down, the Shark spoke. 'Ha, my friend!' he said with another toothy smile, 'I have just had a very amusing experience. When I was in the toilet, I decided to check the messages on my phone. But when I turned it on, I discovered—'

'I have your phone,' Hiro said quickly.

The Shark watched Hiro for a moment, then seemed to relax. Hiro had an odd feeling he'd spoken just in time.

'Yes,' he said, 'and I have yours. Is this your girlfriend?' he went on, giving a short laugh. 'She is very beautiful. What is her name?' The Shark held out Hiro's phone across the table. The screensaver photo of Yuki was showing.

'Yuki,' Hiro answered.

The Shark gave a strange nod of his head. 'A very beautiful dog. How amusing that we have the same kind of Nokia phone! Now perhaps you would return mine?'

Hiro was already holding the phone. He held it out, trying to stop his hand from shaking. 'I'm very sorry,' he said. 'A message came through and I opened it before I realised ...'

The Shark's eyes narrowed. He watched Hiro for a moment. 'Of course you did; that is quite natural,' he said, then looked at his phone. Hiro didn't move while the Shark opened the message. Hiro saw him read it, then close it again. 'Yes, from a business colleague,' the Shark said.

There was silence for a moment or two. Hiro didn't know what to say. Then the Shark slowly nodded his head and smiled. 'So, since we know each other's great secrets, I think we must introduce ourselves. My name is Erik Björnson. I am a businessman from Sweden. And who, may I ask, do I have the pleasure to meet?'

Chapter 4   *A helping hand*

Hiro felt hot. The train seemed to be travelling even faster.

'My name's Hiro Adachi,' he said. 'I'm from Japan.'

'Yes, of course,' the Shark answered. 'Japan is one of my favourite countries,' he went on. As he spoke, he sat forward, held out his hand and smiled. The smile seemed even more frightening than before.

'Pleased to meet you,' Hiro said, taking the man's hand. It felt cold and wet, like the skin of a fish.

'The pleasure is mine,' the Shark replied. 'So, I suppose you are a student taking a holiday?'

'Yes, I'm InterRailing,' replied Hiro.

'Very good. Berlin is your first stop?' the Shark asked.

'Yes,' said Hiro.

'And how many nights will you stay in Berlin? It is a very exciting city,' the Shark continued.

'I'm not sure,' Hiro answered.

The Shark nodded slowly. 'You have already booked a hotel, of course?'

Hiro had an uncomfortable feeling that there was a reason for the questions. He suddenly didn't want to tell the Shark where he was staying. 'Not yet. I was going to look around,' he replied. The Shark's eyes became very small.

'In Kreuzberg maybe,' Hiro added quickly. He wondered if that was enough information to give.

The Shark nodded. 'Perhaps I can suggest somewhere. The Hotel Modena? Cheap, but very comfortable.'

'Thank you so much. Maybe I'll try it,' replied Hiro.

'I shall telephone for you. The owner is an old friend,' the Shark said, reaching for his phone.

Hiro didn't know what to do. 'Thank you, but I'm hoping to meet someone in Kreuzberg … a Japanese friend … from my city,' he said weakly.

There was silence for a moment. It was a lie and Hiro could see the Shark knew it. Hiro felt very hot.

The Shark smiled. 'Of course. It was simply an idea.' He watched Hiro thoughtfully for a few moments, then spoke again. 'I must apologise to you, my friend. There is something terrible I must tell you. I am a very stupid old man. I read some messages on your phone before I understood it was not mine. I imagine you did the same?'

Hiro felt a drop of sweat run out of his hair. The lights in the train suddenly seemed very bright. 'No,' he said. 'Only one. About your meeting at the Brandenburg Gate.'

There was a long silence again. Hiro wanted to brush the sweat from his forehead. The silence seemed to go on forever. Finally, the man gave another smile and looked away.

*   *   *

At Hannover the train was delayed for half an hour, so it was after seven thirty when they reached Berlin. It was a rainy evening and already getting dark, so the lights of the city shone all around. Hiro felt more relaxed. For the rest of the journey the Shark had slept – well, he'd had his eyes closed. Hiro couldn't be certain he was asleep. Hiro felt silly now for thinking so badly of the old man. Obviously, Hiro's imagination had gone wild after reading that thriller. After all, the man was old enough to be his grandfather – how could anyone like that be dangerous?

Finally they pulled into the station, a huge modern building. Hiro picked up his bag and stood up. Although he felt better, he wanted to get away from the old man as quickly as possible.

'It was very nice to meet you,' Hiro said politely.

The Shark also got up. 'How will you get to Kreuzberg?' he asked.

'I'm going to take the U-Bahn,' Hiro said.

'No, no, that is not good. I shall show you the best way.'

Hiro's heart raced. 'It's very kind of you, but I'll be fine.'

The Shark took Hiro's arm. 'It is no problem.'

Hiro felt the Shark's hand lead him forward, off the train. The platform was busy, but Hiro suddenly felt very alone. Even though he'd persuaded himself that his fears were just the result of a stupid book, Hiro realised he was shaking a little. Here he was in a foreign city, where he didn't speak the language, and this old man was making him afraid.

'Follow me,' the Shark said. 'I will take you to the S-Bahn, to the correct platform, then leave you there.'

Hiro knew he couldn't argue. He tried to keep calm. 'This will be all right,' he told himself. 'In five minutes I'll be on my own again.'

The Shark led the way along the platform until they came to an escalator going down. 'You must take the S-Bahn to Friedrichstrasse,' he said as they stepped together on to the moving escalator. 'It is the next stop. Then you will take the U-Bahn to Hallesches Tor in Kreuzberg. Do you understand?'

The Shark's face was close to Hiro's; his teeth were bright in the station lights.

'Thank you. Yes,' Hiro replied.

They walked across a wide hall. A family of Japanese were standing under a big clock. Hiro thought of calling out to them for help, but couldn't think what to say. A moment later he had passed them and it was too late in any case.

They reached another escalator. This time they went up. The Shark didn't speak. Hiro told himself, 'Only another couple of minutes, then I'll be safe.'

They came out on to another platform. It was wide, but quite crowded near the escalator.

'Come, there is more room further down,' the Shark said.

'I'll be fine now, thank you,' Hiro said.

'No, I shall wait,' the Shark answered. 'I must be sure you take the correct train.'

They stopped two thirds of the way along the platform. It was less wide just there because of a large seat. They were standing quite close to the edge. The sound of a train made Hiro turn around. It was coming in fast. He saw the lights on the front, the driver looking out. Hiro felt the Shark move in closer to him.

The next moment Hiro had a sudden idea of what might happen. Everyone on the platform was looking forward, watching the train. No one was looking in their direction. The Shark was going to push him. He was going to push him off the platform in front of the train!

At the last second Hiro moved back from the edge of the platform. At the same time the Shark seemed to reach out as if he was falling. Hiro felt the Shark take his arm, but Hiro was now away from the danger. The next moment the train had raced past. The scream of brakes followed. A few seconds later the train had come to a stop.

Chapter 5 *A difficult decision*

'Please! You frightened me! You nearly fell!' the Shark said.

Hiro stared in fear, unable to speak. The old man's face was close to Hiro's and he was holding his arm very tightly.

'You must not stand so close to the edge of the platform!' the Shark went on. 'But this is your train. Climb in quickly!' He moved even closer to Hiro. 'Take great care, young man. Leave Berlin alive – not in a coffin!'

Their eyes met for a second, then Hiro felt the Shark give him a push. A moment later Hiro found himself inside the train, the electric doors closing behind him.

Almost immediately the train began to pull out of the station. Hiro couldn't move. He stood in the doorway, looking at the Shark outside on the platform. The old man didn't move either, but watched Hiro all the time as the train pulled away. Then the train left the bright lights of the station and the Shark disappeared from view.

At last Hiro was alone. Without thinking, he fell into a seat. Suddenly he realised he was wet with sweat. He undid his jacket. Was he dreaming or had the Shark really tried to kill him? It seemed a completely crazy idea, but Hiro couldn't think of any other explanation. The Shark had led him to the edge of the platform, he'd moved behind Hiro, then reached out and caught his arm. And what was that final thing he'd said? 'Leave Berlin alive – not in a coffin!' Wasn't a coffin the wooden box they use for dead bodies? Hiro suddenly felt very cold. He stared out through the train window at the city, but saw nothing except the Shark's cold grey eyes looking back at him.

How he reached his hotel that night, Hiro never knew. It was like a terrible dream. When he thought about it later, he had a memory of getting off the train at Friedrichstrasse and following a group of other travellers down into the U-Bahn. He couldn't remember anything of that underground journey except hearing 'Hallesches Tor!' After that he somehow made his way through the streets in the darkness, following the map in his guidebook. But he remembered the little old man, Herr Albert, who opened the door of the Hotel Alma when Hiro pressed the bell. Herr Albert had taken Hiro up to the second floor in an old lift with metal gates and wooden doors. That evening the hotel seemed like a second home to Hiro and Herr Albert like a second father. Hiro fell into bed and was asleep only a few seconds later.

* * *

When Hiro woke the next morning, everything came back to him immediately. There seemed to be no escape from the awful dream. The moment he opened his eyes it felt as if the Shark was standing next to the bed and whispering, 'Leave Berlin alive – not in a coffin!'

Hiro's first idea was to catch the earliest train out of the city. He would go directly to Prague, or maybe Warsaw or Amsterdam – anywhere as long as he could get out of Berlin.

But then, as Hiro lay in bed looking up at the ceiling, thinking about what had happened on the platform, he started to feel angry. 'Why should an old man make me run off?' he thought. Hiro began to wonder why he'd been so afraid. Perhaps it was because he was safe inside his hotel room, but Hiro thought he should teach the Shark a lesson. He would show him who was boss!

Hiro felt confused, but the longer he lay there, the angrier he became. If the Shark had really tried to push him off the platform, then that was … Hiro sat up, his blood boiling. Who was this man who called himself Erik Björnson? If he had really wanted to kill Hiro, it must be because of the messages Hiro had read on his phone. There was one idea that Hiro couldn't get out of his mind – the Shark was a killer. And the messages meant that he was planning to kill someone that night. Hiro had to do something. But what?

He thought about Akiko. She always knew what to do. For a moment he considered phoning her, but then he stopped himself. No, when Akiko had said she didn't want to hear from him, he'd replied, 'Don't worry, you won't!' He wouldn't be the weak one. If she decided to phone him, well, that was different. Hiro jumped up from the bed, angry that he'd even considered the idea for a second.

When Hiro went into breakfast, Herr Albert gave him a friendly wave and took him to a table. At one table a young American couple were discussing a boat trip on the Wannsee. Hiro ate some cereal, thinking how good it would be to have such an uncomplicated stay in the city. All of a sudden he realised that Herr Albert was at his shoulder.

'You would like an egg?' Herr Albert was asking softly.

'I'm sorry,' Hiro answered. 'No, no egg, thank you,' Then, without knowing he was about to say it, he went on, 'Could you tell me where the nearest police station is?'

Chapter 6   *A visit to the police station*

Half an hour later, Hiro was outside the police station at Hallesches Tor. Looking up at the building he felt his new confidence suddenly leave him. It was a huge grey place with very few windows and, standing there, Hiro began to feel nervous. He thought about the lie he had told Herr Albert – that his camera had been stolen and he wanted to report it. How he wished that was true. How he wished that he had never met the Shark and that all he had to worry about was a missing camera. Suddenly it seemed like a big mistake to come to the police. He wasn't even certain any more that the Shark had tried to kill him.

From the start it didn't go well. The first police officer he spoke to could understand very little English, and immediately called for someone else. Hiro waited nervously for half an hour in the crowded waiting room, watching people come and go.

At last, a woman police officer in a bright green and white uniform appeared. She introduced herself as Petra Müller, and led Hiro off to a small glass-walled office at the back of the police station.

Hiro began badly. 'I think an old man tried to kill me,' he said. At that, the police officer raised her eyebrows. 'I read some messages on this man's phone. I think he's going to murder someone tonight in the Hotel Adlon,' Hiro continued. 'And then he tried to push me off the platform in front of a train.' The words came falling out of Hiro's mouth. Within half a minute, he was in a terrible mess.

'All right,' the police officer said quietly. 'Perhaps we should take this a bit more slowly.' Hiro had to repeat himself while the police officer took several pages of notes. Then she finally stood up and told Hiro she was going to get someone else.

It was half an hour before she reappeared, this time with an older man, who was fat and smelt strongly of cigarettes. He wasn't wearing a uniform and Hiro decided he must be a detective. The detective didn't introduce himself. He sat on the table and crossed his arms.

'So, you're the Japanese boy who thinks an old man has tried to kill him. Is that correct?' the detective started.

Hiro didn't know how to answer.

'Is that correct?' the detective repeated.

'Yes, that's right,' Hiro said at last.

'And why do you believe this old man wished to murder you?' the detective asked.

Hiro felt more nervous all the time. 'I explained to your colleague that—'

'I don't wish to know what you explained to my colleague. I want you to tell me!' the detective said angrily. Hiro looked up at the detective. He seemed to be in a very bad mood – as if he would start shouting at any moment.

'By accident I read some messages on the old man's phone,' Hiro said quietly. 'We were on the train and I picked up his phone by mistake.'

'Yes, yes, I know all that,' the detective said impatiently. 'What I want to know is why you believe an old man would wish to kill you for that!'

Hiro smelt cigarettes on the detective's breath again. 'I think the messages I read on the old man's phone were very important,' Hiro said quietly. 'One message said he had an assignment at the Hotel Adlon.'

The detective's eyes lit up. 'Ah, an assignment! He smiled at the woman police officer. 'I'm sorry. Go on.'

Hiro felt hot. 'And the other message said he was going to collect half his fee and some equipment today at—'

'Equipment, eh!' the detective broke in. 'And what do you think is meant by that?'

'I'm not sure,' Hiro said nervously. 'I thought …' Hiro came to a stop.

'Well?' the detective said.

'I'm not sure,' Hiro answered. 'I thought it might be a gun,' he said at last, dropping his head.

There was silence. Hiro could feel the detective's eyes on him. Finally, the man got up from the table and began to walk round the room. 'OK, let's leave all that for the moment. Now, you say he tried to kill you. How exactly did he do that?'

'We were on the platform at the main station,' Hiro explained. 'He was standing behind me. I think he was going to push me.'

'You *think* he was going to push you.' The detective said the words slowly.

'Yes, and he got hold of my arm,' Hiro went on.

'And he got hold of your arm,' the detective repeated after him.

There was silence. Hiro felt his face going red. Now that he'd said out loud what he believed, it suddenly seemed very stupid. He saw the detective watching him. The man just gave a tired nod. Then he spoke.

'I guess you like spy films, yes? James Bond, Jason Bourne, this sort of rubbish?'

Hiro didn't look up.

'You know, I suppose, that it's a very serious business to waste police time,' the detective went on.

'Yes, I do,' Hiro answered.

'And you can imagine how busy we are,' the detective said.

Hiro nodded. There was silence again.

The detective went on at last. 'What are you doing here in Berlin alone?'

'I'm on an InterRail trip,' Hiro replied.

'I know. But why are you by yourself? Where are your friends?' the detective asked.

'I … I was going to have a holiday with my girlfriend, but … we've just broken up,' Hiro said quietly.

'Ah! So now we have it. A broken heart!' The detective shook his head and walked over to the door. 'Look, my friend,' he said, 'Nobody is trying to kill you, and there aren't going to be any murders in the Hotel Adlon tonight. You're living in a dream. You see one thing and you imagine another. It's all in your mind. Now, return to your hotel, pack your bags and get a train back to England as fast as you can. Buy your girlfriend some flowers, that's my advice.'

With that, he hurried out of the door, calling some orders in German to the woman police officer as he left the room.

Hiro looked down at the floor. He had never before felt so small.

Chapter 7 *Painful thoughts*

When Hiro got back to his hotel, he went to his room, lay down on the bed and didn't move for a long time.

He felt terrible. The police hadn't believed him. Worse than that, they'd made him feel like a schoolboy again, a schoolboy who dreamt of spy stories and cried over the girlfriend he'd lost.

The visit to the police station made him remember something that had happened when he was about thirteen. It wasn't a happy memory. One very snowy day on his way to school, Hiro saw a man breaking the side window of a car. The man got in and drove off. Hiro quickly wrote down the number of the car, then called 110, the emergency number of the police. All day Hiro felt very proud of what he'd done and told all his school friends. But that evening Hiro's father took a call from the police. The man who had 'stolen' the car was its owner. The locks on the car had frozen and he'd needed his car in an emergency. Hiro felt very stupid and never told any of his friends the end of the story.

Now he had the same feeling. What had the detective said about seeing one thing and imagining another? Hiro wouldn't tell anyone about his visit to the police that morning and he would never again ask them for help.

After half an hour of such thoughts, Hiro suddenly jumped up from the bed. Lying there like that, reliving the past and feeling sorry for himself, was weak. That was schoolboy behaviour – just like keeping all those love messages from Akiko on his phone. Immediately, he picked up his phone, went to Akiko's texts, and prepared to delete them. His hand shook for a second or two. 'Delete all messages?' appeared on the screen. With a little cry of pain, he pressed the 'OK' key.

After that, Hiro put on his jacket and hurried out of his room, almost knocking over Herr Albert, who was cleaning the corridor. He went down in the old wooden lift and quickly out into the street. He had no idea where he was going or what he was going to do, but the sun was shining now. He tried to tell himself he was happier.

He stopped in a small café a short way up the road, and asked for a green tea. He took his cup and went to sit by the window. Looking out, watching all the people passing, his head began to feel clearer. He tried to decide what to do. As he was on holiday, Hiro thought he really ought to do some sightseeing. He took out his guidebook and started to read.

The very first place he found, on the first page of the guidebook, was the Brandenburg Gate. Hiro stared at the picture. The words seemed to jump out of the page at him: 'The Brandenburg Gate, Berlin's most famous sight, is in Pariser Platz, where the famous Hotel Adlon can also be found.' The Brandenburg Gate … the Hotel Adlon. Hiro read the words again, then looked at his watch. It was twelve o'clock. In one hour the Shark would be at his meeting; he would collect the gun and get the first half of his fee.

Hiro had a sick feeling in his stomach. His heart had started to beat very fast. He closed his eyes. When he opened them again, he knew what he must do. He'd found the strength to delete Akiko's messages, now he had to be brave again. If the police wouldn't go to the Brandenburg Gate, he would have to do it himself. There was just time to get there before one o'clock.

Immediately, he pushed his tea away and hurried across the café. He almost threw a five-euro note across the counter. He didn't wait for any change. There wasn't a moment to lose.

He found a U-Bahn station just round the corner and stopped at the map inside the entrance. Which was the way to go? He needed to get to Unter den Linden – that was the nearest stop to the Brandenburg Gate. It seemed very complicated: he would have to travel up to Friedrichstrasse and then get a different line. Remembering what his guidebook said, he hurried into a newspaper shop to buy a train ticket, then ran down to the platform.

At least he didn't have to wait long. Soon a train arrived and he jumped in. He went to stand against the opposite door, too nervous and excited to sit down.

The journey seemed endless, although it wasn't more than five stops. Then he was running along the platform and up and down the stairs to get to the other line.

This time there was a longer wait. He had just missed a train. It was already 12.40 – only twenty minutes before the Shark's meeting. Hiro walked up and down the platform.

At 12.45 the train appeared at last. The moment it stopped Hiro opened the door and jumped inside. It was only one stop now, three or four minutes, no more. He tried to calm himself down, take some deep breaths. The train pulled out of the station and raced into the darkness. Surely now he must be there in time?

Chapter 8 *A little bit of sightseeing*

When Hiro came out of the underground station five minutes later, he found himself in a wide street. Smart shops and hotels stretched away in both directions – and there was the Brandenburg Gate, a couple of hundred metres away. Hiro saw the six columns of the great Greek-style gateway, just as he'd seen in the guidebook, and on its top, the horses and chariot against the sky.

Hiro made his way towards the Gate. It was 12.50. Now he had to take great care. He would have to get close to the Gate if he wanted to see the Shark's meeting take place. But he also had to make sure he kept out of sight. He must make sure the Shark didn't see him.

At first there was no problem. Cars were parked all the way up the street and Hiro kept close to these. On the left-hand side he noticed the entrance to the Hotel Adlon, a grand building with a revolving door. If Hiro was right, it was there that evening the Shark would complete his work.

Further up the street it became more difficult. The street opened up into a wide square – the Pariser Platz. Now Hiro could be seen more easily. But there were plenty of cars here too, many of them very large, with dark windows. He walked past these, getting closer all the time to the Gate. Now he could see how big it was. There were lots of people wandering about around the columns. He didn't know what to do. Perhaps the Shark would meet his friend on the other side of the Gate, where most of the tourists were. But to get close was so dangerous! It was 12.55. If only he weren't so easy to notice. If only he weren't Japanese!

A coach pulling up on the far side of the Gate caught his eye. After a few moments, the passengers came pouring out of its door. Hiro had an idea. The tourists were all Europeans or Americans, but if he could get round to that side, a coach full of Japanese tourists was sure to appear soon. He began to make his way round.

Hiro was nearly there, when just as he'd guessed, a coach pulled up by the side of the road. Almost immediately thirty or forty Japanese tourists of all ages came hurrying down the steps. Hiro went to join them.

The sound of his own language made him want to cry out, but he stopped himself. He had to look out for the Shark. Several of the group hurried forward, pulling cameras from cases, and Hiro moved with them. As he got nearer the Gate his eyes searched the foot of the columns. He couldn't see the Shark. He looked at his watch. It was exactly one o'clock.

Hiro studied the people round the Gate. Several were wandering around, looking up at the columns or standing for photographs, but none of them looked anything like the Shark. The only person over fifty years old was a priest, wearing long black clothes, standing away to the left. Hiro felt disappointed. After fighting his fears so bravely, was it all for nothing? Hiro watched as the priest was joined by a second man. The two of them went off behind one of the columns and disappeared from view.

Five minutes passed. Hiro began to wonder if he'd made a mistake. Should he go back to the other side of the Gate?

An old man walking with a stick came slowly past. Hiro's heart missed a beat. He couldn't see the man's face. Was this the Shark, pretending to need a stick? Hiro moved in order to see the man's face, but then stopped. A little old woman, perhaps eighty years of age, had joined the old man.

Hiro shook his head and looked at his watch: 1.10. Was the Shark really not coming? Hiro began to consider the possibilities. What if, following the mix-up with the phones, the Shark had changed the time or place of the meeting?

A hand on his shoulder made Hiro jump. For a second he thought it must be the Shark. Then he gave a sick laugh. One of the Japanese women from the coach was smiling at him and holding out her camera. She wanted Hiro to take a photo of her and her friend in front of the Gate, and she was speaking in Japanese. Hiro felt stupid – he'd been in such a dream that he hadn't even recognised his own language. He took the photo as asked, handed back the camera, and looked at his watch. It was 1.20.

So, the Shark wasn't coming after all. Hiro felt very stupid. 'Perhaps the detective at the police station was right,' he thought. 'Perhaps I should just take the first train back to England.' He walked straight towards the Gate, no longer hiding among the Japanese tourists, and headed for the underground station. He just wanted to get out of Berlin now, to get out of this stupid city.

Hiro was less than fifty metres from the underground station, when the sound of a car close behind him made him look round. A black BMW with dark windows stopped beside him. As it did so, the back window opened and a dark-haired man looked out.

'Mr Hiro Adachi?' the man asked in English. He didn't wait for an answer. 'I'd like a word with you. It's very important.'

Chapter 9 *The safe house*

Hiro looked inside the car. 'Yes?' he said. He was too surprised to say anything else.

'My name is Karl Meier,' the man went on. He was very smartly dressed. 'I work for the *Bundesnachrichtendienst.* The BND is a department of the German police. Foreign intelligence. We need to talk to you. Get in, please.'

At the same moment the driver of the car climbed out. His head was shaved and he wore a black leather jacket. He looked very tough. He opened the back door for Hiro.

Hiro felt his heart beat fast. 'Yes, of course,' he said. He was feeling very nervous, not sure if he should get in, but the driver put his hand on Hiro's shoulder. Hiro climbed into the car next to Karl Meier. Almost immediately, the driver banged the door shut, got in the front and the car pulled away. It had all happened so quickly, Hiro couldn't think.

'Don't worry, my friend,' Meier said. 'You're quite safe with us.' He put out his hand. 'I'm very pleased to meet you, Mr Adachi. You're a very brave young man.'

Hiro shook the man's hand. The car had already left Unter den Linden and was racing through the streets. Hiro saw the driver watching him in the mirror. He had a long cut on his face.

'Where are we going?' Hiro asked Karl Meier.

'Just somewhere we can talk more quietly, Mr Adachi.' The man gave a strange smile. In the car mirror, Hiro saw the driver smile, too. Hiro began to feel uncomfortable. How could the police have known where he was? He wished he hadn't got into the car now. Why hadn't one of the men shown him a police card or something?

The car raced on. No one spoke. Hiro had no idea where they were.

At last Hiro managed to find his voice. 'How did you know where to find me?' he said with a cough.

Meier didn't look at him. 'We've been following you for some time,' he said quietly.

Hiro saw the driver smile once again.

'You mean since I went to the police station this morning?' Hiro asked.

Meier looked round at that. He watched Hiro for a moment or two, then nodded very gently. 'Yes, that's right. There are some things you said which we want to double-check.'

Hiro did his best to relax. At least he had an explanation now for how they'd picked him up.

At last they turned into a small street and drove round to the back of a large building. Hiro wasn't sure if it was offices or flats. Then the car pulled over the pavement and went down into an underground car park. The car headlights shone brightly in the darkness. Hiro felt a little sick.

They came to a stop opposite a lift. Immediately, the driver got out and told Hiro to follow him. Hiro climbed out of the car and a moment later, Meier joined them.

'This is what we call a "safe house",' Meier said. 'We use it for interviews, among other things. Naturally, we can't take most people to our head office. Please follow me.'

Meier led the way over to the lift, pressed a button on the wall and the doors opened immediately. The three of them went inside. It was dirty and smelly. An empty beer can was lying on the floor. With a tired look, Meier kicked it away.

The lift went slowly up, then the doors opened. When they stepped out there were two brown doors in front of them, a long corridor leading off to the right, and stairs up and down.

The driver took a key from his pocket, unlocked the door on the left, then Meier led the way inside. Hiro relaxed a little when he saw it was a simple flat. There was a bedroom and bathroom off to one side of the hall, a kitchen directly ahead and a lounge to the right. They went into the lounge and Meier turned on the light. There was very little furniture: a sofa and two armchairs, a coffee table, a TV, but it seemed no one lived there. There were no pictures on the wall, and there was nothing very warm about the room. Meier sat in one of the armchairs.

'Please have a seat,' he said pointing to the sofa. 'Would you like a coffee, perhaps?' he added.

'No, thank you,' Hiro answered.

Meier spoke quickly in German to the driver, who went off into the kitchen. Hiro didn't like the feeling in the room. It was cold and strange.

Meier seemed in a hurry to start. 'So, when you went to the police this morning, the ordinary police, that is—'

'I thought they hadn't believed me,' Hiro broke in.

Meier's eyes narrowed. 'Yes, you're right. They're very stupid people. The truth is that your report was picked up on our computer. We acted immediately.'

'I see,' Hiro answered, a little uncertainly.

Meier looked uncomfortable. 'Right, now it's important that you tell me in your own words what you told the ordinary police. You told them about the old man on the train, of course. And what did you tell them about the messages that you read on his phone?' Meier was sitting forward now and looking very closely at Hiro. Hiro didn't answer. This is all wrong, he thought. The men are wrong, the room is wrong, the questions are wrong. He didn't know what to do.

'So?' said Meier impatiently.

Hiro looked at the man. 'I'm sorry. Is there a toilet I could use, please?'

Meier looked annoyed for a moment, then seemed to relax. 'Yes, of course,' he said with a smile. 'I'll show you.'

'Thank you,' Hiro replied.

Meier led Hiro out of the room and opened the bathroom door for him. Hiro went in and closed the door. He heard Meier go off into the kitchen and start talking to the driver. Hiro sat on the edge of the bath and put his head in his hands. He had to think. 'These men aren't real policemen, or foreign intelligence,' he said to himself. 'They must be friends of the Shark. Perhaps they followed me from the Brandenburg Gate. Yes, that must be it! Maybe the Shark *had* been at the Gate earlier. He'd met these men there. When they saw me they decided to follow me and pick me up. So what are they going to do with me now?'

Hiro looked around. He had to escape. There was no way out of the bathroom except through the door. What could he do?

He got up, went over to the door and listened. He could hear Meier talking in German. It sounded as though he had returned to the lounge. Maybe he was talking on the phone.

Hiro's brain was racing. He thought: 'They want to be sure what I know.' That was why Meier was asking the questions and not the Shark – by pretending to be police they hoped to get more information from him. If the Shark asked the questions, Hiro might refuse to talk. But once they'd heard everything, surely they would kill him. 'It'll be a shot in the back of the head,' Hiro told himself. 'Either that, or a fall from the window, perhaps.'

There was no time to think about it any more. Hiro looked round the bathroom once more. Then he made a decision. He had one chance only. If he was going to escape it had to be now.

He stood by the door.

Chapter 10 *Escape!*

Very carefully, Hiro opened the bathroom door and put his head out into the hall. He'd been right – Meier was back in the lounge. He was talking on his phone, looking down, deep in conversation. The driver was out of sight in the kitchen.

Hiro took a deep breath. He had only a few seconds to get to the front door. He took off his shoes and quietly crossed the hall. Five steps only and he was at the front door. If the door was locked, he was finished …

He was in luck. With a tiny sound, the door opened, then he was out into the main corridor. He ran straight to the stairs.

He went down only three or four steps before he realised he was making a mistake. 'No,' he thought, 'Once they realise I've gone, they'll expect me to go down, so I must go up instead.' He turned and ran back up the steps two at a time. He'd just managed to reach the next floor when he heard the men run out of the flat, shouting in German. He heard them stop outside the lift.

Hiro could only guess what they were shouting, but then he heard their footsteps hurrying down the stairs.

So, what to do now? Hiro's heart was racing. In a short time the men would realise he hadn't gone down and they would fly back up the steps. A fire escape! There had to be a fire escape in a place like this. But where?

He ran up two floors without stopping, still carrying his shoes. Then he was at the top – there were no more stairs, just another corridor. Far below he could hear the men shouting. Then silence. They were listening for him. Listening for his footsteps. Then Hiro heard one of them coming up.

There was nothing for it. Hiro ran the length of the corridor. At the end of the corridor there was a door. He pushed and the door opened.

Hiro found himself outside on a fire escape, a metal staircase going down the outside of the building. Should he go down? He had no choice. At any moment the man coming up would look along the corridor and see him.

Hiro went down a couple of steps, then heard a door opening somewhere below. He ran back up and watched as the driver came out on to the fire escape two floors below him. Hiro saw him look down, then, just as the man was about to look up, Hiro pressed himself back against the wall. His heart was beating crazily. Surely the man would see him! Two or three seconds passed. Then Hiro heard the man shout back into the building before he went inside and the door banged shut. Hiro took another deep breath. He was out of danger!

Hiro was just about to start down the steps, when something stopped him again. Was it a tiny sound from below or something else? The memory of something from a film came back to him. It had been a trick! The driver's shout had been a trick to make Hiro think the way was safe – the man had closed the door loudly, but he was still outside on the fire escape at that moment, looking up. Hiro didn't move. He closed his eyes. Akiko's face came to his mind. 'Please help me,' he said softly. Ten long seconds passed, then there was a quiet call from below. After that the door closed again. This time Hiro knew the man had really gone inside.

Hiro's legs were shaking as he made his way down the stairs. He didn't stop now or look around. The only thing he thought about was getting to the bottom. He almost fell once, but managed to stop himself, then in thirty seconds he was down on the ground.

He found himself on a small path between buildings. One way led to the main street at the front of the building. He could see people walking past. That was the way to go. Hiro walked quickly towards the street. Just as he got there, he saw a bus pull up about ten metres down the road. He didn't stop to think, but ran towards it. He reached the bus just as the driver was about to close the doors. Hiro almost threw himself inside and fell on to a seat.

As the bus pulled away, Hiro saw Meier appear through the glass door of the building he'd just left. Hiro dropped his head from view, pretending to tie up his shoes. It was another couple of minutes before he was brave enough to raise his head and look around. When he did, he took out his phone and opened his photo of Akiko. '*Arigato,*' he whispered. 'Thank you.' Then, under his breath, 'I'm so sorry I deleted your messages. It was a terrible mistake.'

Chapter 11 *The eye of the storm*

Ten minutes later the bus pulled into a huge modern square and stopped. Most of the passengers hurried off. Not wanting to be alone anywhere now, Hiro followed them. He felt safer where there were crowds of people, and this place was busy with shoppers. Even so, he couldn't stop himself looking back every ten seconds or so. Had Meier seen him take the bus and guessed where it was going?

To one side of the square there was a wall where a number of people were sitting. There was a kebab-seller nearby and most of the people on the wall were eating snacks. They looked relaxed and cheerful, chatting and taking photographs of one another. Hiro went over and sat down in the middle of them. Being Japanese he knew he could be easily noticed, but with so many people around surely he wasn't in danger?

Once he'd sat down, Hiro realised how terribly tired he was. His first thought was to return to his hotel and just fall on the bed. It would be so wonderful to sleep again untroubled. He felt as though he'd been living in fear of his life for weeks. Was it really only twenty-four hours since he met the Shark?

A cinema sign on the far side of the square caught Hiro's eye. All of a sudden the idea of sitting in the darkness, safe from the world for a couple of hours, seemed wonderful. It would be like the calm time in the middle of the storm. What did they call it – the eye? Without wasting another moment, he got up and hurried over to the cinema entrance. He couldn't stop himself from looking behind as he went, but no one appeared to be following him.

When he arrived at the box office, he discovered he was in luck. A new thriller was about to start. He paid, bought a hotdog and went through to find a seat.

Some advertisements were showing when he went in, but it was beautifully dark. Still worried that someone may be following him, he chose a seat right at the back. In that way, he thought, he could see everyone who entered. He sat down and immediately began eating the hotdog. He hadn't thought about food since breakfast and was surprised to find how hungry he was.

Very soon the film started. Thankfully, it was in English and not German. All the same, it made Hiro feel exhausted; everyone spoke very quickly and Hiro found it hard to follow. He started thinking about what had happened that day. He had to find the answers to some questions.

Hiro was absolutely certain now that the Shark was an assassin – a professional killer. The old man had come to Berlin to kill someone. The text message had said, 'Berlin Assignment Hotel Adlon Room 319 Tuesday after 8pm', so the murder was to take place that evening in Room 319 of the Hotel Adlon. He supposed the Shark had been at the Brandenburg Gate after all, probably with Meier. When they saw Hiro there, they'd decided Meier would follow him. They wanted to know if the police knew about the Hotel Adlon. If they did, then the Shark might have to cancel his plan. Yes, that must be it! So what about the murder? Would it still go ahead? And what should Hiro do?

Hiro felt so tired thinking about all these questions and worrying about what to do. It seemed to him that the trip had become some kind of test. He remembered something his grandfather had said to him, shortly before he died. The old man was very ill and had only a few days to live, so the whole family had come to say goodbye. Taking Hiro by the arm, the old man had pulled Hiro close to the bed. 'Life is an examination, Hiro-chan,' he said. 'Make me proud.' Those words rang in Hiro's ears now. Is this what the old man meant? Hiro shook his head, exhausted, and closed his eyes. The film music washed over him like waves on the beach.

The next thing Hiro knew, a man in a white shirt and black tie had his arm on Hiro's shoulder. The man was shaking him hard. The man said something in German, then tried in English: 'Hey! No sleeping here!'

Hiro shook his head. 'What?' he said. He couldn't understand where he was. Then he remembered.

'No sleeping!' The man in the white shirt was still shaking him. 'Go to a hotel if you want to sleep!'

Hiro pulled himself up. 'I'm sorry.'

The man gave an angry look, but moved away, collecting rubbish from the seats.

Hiro looked at his watch: 5.45! He couldn't believe it. He must have slept through the rest of the film.

He got to his feet. Then the full memory of the last twenty-four hours hit him: the Shark … the Brandenburg Gate … Meier and the safe house …

Hiro fell back in the seat and put his hands to his head.

Chapter 12 *A voice in the ear*

It was almost six o'clock when Hiro left the cinema. There were dark clouds in the sky and all around the square the lights from advertisements shone as brightly as if it were night. For a moment Hiro thought he could be back in Tokyo. It made him feel terribly homesick. But he wasn't at home. A sign above the cinema read: 'Alexanderplatz'. He looked at the map in his guidebook to see where he was.

Alexanderplatz wasn't difficult to find on the map. He saw he wasn't very far from his hotel – only seven or eight stops on the U-Bahn. Without thinking, Hiro walked towards the U-Bahn entrance. He didn't have much idea what he was going to do when he got back to his hotel room. He supposed he was just going to lie on the bed and read or watch TV until he was able to sleep. Then he would leave Berlin the following morning. His trip seemed a failure, but he'd had enough. He felt frightened and tired and cold. Hadn't he done all he could? He'd been brave and put himself in danger – his grandfather couldn't be disappointed with him. Why shouldn't Hiro just quietly leave Berlin now and go somewhere else?

Alexanderplatz station was big and busy. There seemed to be several lines, both overground and underground – he checked the map again and chose U-Bahn 2. He would have to change trains once.

He didn't have to wait long for a train. He climbed in and sat in the corner. The train was very full. Looking up and down he watched all the different men and women, old and young, rich and poor. Some were clearly on their way home from work, others were just starting out for the evening. He watched a couple of his age, talking closely together and sharing a quick kiss. How wonderful, he thought. How lovely it must be to have so few cares in the world. The stations hurried by one after another. Dreamily, Hiro watched the lively city passing before his eyes.

It was only when they pulled into Potsdamer Platz that Hiro realised he'd missed his station. Looking at the map on the inside of the train he saw that he had forgotten to get out earlier and change to U-Bahn 6. With a shake of his head, he jumped up and went to the door.

Just before stepping out of the train, he stopped. 'Why shouldn't I just continue the journey?' he thought. 'I could go on to the end of the line and get the train back. It would at least kill some time.'

With a smile he went back to his seat. The woman sitting in the next seat seemed surprised. The train pulled out. Hiro looked at his watch: 6.35. He tried to relax.

Five minutes later he knew it was impossible. He couldn't sit still. He couldn't simply go back to his hotel and pretend he knew nothing of the Shark's plans. A voice was whispering in his ear. The voice had started the moment Hiro had decided to go back to his hotel room. 'Coward!' it was saying. 'You're not brave at all. You're being a coward!'

With each station that passed the feeling grew worse. He looked at his watch again. It was 6.45 now. It hit him then – in about an hour's time it was quite possible that a murder would take place! Hiro began to feel very sick. He was the only person who knew about the Shark's plans. He was the only person who might stop them. He had to go back. He had to do something. When the train pulled into the next station, Hiro was already waiting at the door to go back.

*   *   *

It was 7.15 when Hiro reached Unter den Linden. While Hiro had been down in the underground it had started to rain outside. Cars drove past down the wide street, their wheels throwing up showers of water. Hiro buttoned up his jacket and set off for the Hotel Adlon. Beyond he could see the Brandenburg Gate. Now it was evening, the columns were lit with a strange golden light; the whole place looked very foreign and frightening.

When he arrived at the entrance of the Hotel Adlon, Hiro was nervous. A doorman stood outside the big revolving door. He was just moving forward with an umbrella to welcome someone arriving in a large silver Mercedes. The woman who climbed out of the back of the Mercedes was beautiful and dressed in very expensive clothes. Hiro stood to the side as she walked past him and into the hotel. As the revolving door turned around and around he could see bright lights and a shiny floor inside the hotel. It was so grand – Hiro had never been in a hotel like it before. He took a deep breath and went through the revolving door himself.

Over to one side there were several beautiful brown leather sofas and armchairs. A well-dressed young man was working at a laptop in one of the armchairs. On a sofa an older couple in evening clothes were chatting.

Hiro went over to the reception desk. The receptionist, a smartly-dressed young man with glasses, looked very surprised when he saw Hiro. He spoke to him in German.

Hiro cleared his throat. 'Do you speak English, please?'

The receptionist looked very doubtful about Hiro. Hiro knew what the man must think of him. Hiro was a poorly-dressed student standing at the desk of a five-star hotel. 'Of course,' the receptionist answered in perfect English. 'How may I help you?'

Hiro tried to speak in a strong voice. 'I'd like to see the manager, please.'

The receptionist gave a small nod. 'The manager is expecting you, of course …?'

'No,' Hiro said.

The receptionist smiled weakly. 'Then I'm afraid I must ask you to arrange a meeting by telephone or email. I'm sure the manager will be very happy to see you then.'

Hiro tried to keep calm. His heart was beating hard. 'It's extremely important,' he said. 'I really must see the manager now.'

The receptionist smiled again and pressed a button at the side of the desk.

Hiro felt the bright lights burning down on his head. He was hot and exhausted. 'Please listen to me,' he said hopelessly. 'This really is an emergency!'

The receptionist continued to smile. Out of the corner of his eye, Hiro saw a man in uniform coming over.

'You must listen to me,' Hiro said, almost crying. 'There's going to be a murder here this evening! Please, you must believe me! Someone is planning to kill one of your guests!'

Chapter 13   *Last hope!*

Five minutes later Hiro was sitting at a table in a small office at the back of the hotel. The man in uniform was standing at the door. His arms were crossed and he looked angry. Hiro felt almost like a prisoner in a cell. He supposed the man at the door imagined he might try to run out of the room. Perhaps he thought he would behave badly and embarrass the guests. Hiro guessed that was the only reason he was not out on the street.

After a couple of minutes, another man appeared in the doorway. He was very smartly dressed, like the receptionist, and also wore glasses, but his hair was going grey at the sides. With a nod, he came round the table and sat opposite Hiro.

'Good evening,' he said. He didn't offer to shake hands. 'My name is Herr Fischer. I'm the duty manager here tonight. Could you tell me your name, please?'

'Adachi,' Hiro answered, politely dropping his head. 'Hiro Adachi.'

'From Japan?' the duty manager asked.

'Yes, I'm a student on a Study Year Abroad programme in England,' Hiro went on. 'I'm here in Berlin on holiday.'

'Excellent.' Fischer put his hands together very calmly on the table. 'Now, please could you explain what you told the receptionist? I understand you told him …' The man paused. 'You told him something unpleasant would happen in the hotel tonight.'

Hiro knew he had to remain calm. If he seemed in any way crazy now, everything would be lost. 'Yes,' Hiro said. 'I'd better tell you immediately. I went to the police this morning, but they didn't believe me. But what I told them is completely true. Honestly!'

'I see …' Fischer gave another patient nod.

'You see I discovered someone is planning a murder here in Room 319 this evening – it could be any time after eight o'clock. That's why it's an emergency.'

'Yes, I completely understand. But perhaps you'd better start from the beginning?' Fischer gave a weak smile.

Hiro nodded. 'Of course.' He began his story. He tried to tell it slowly and calmly, but from time to time it became impossible. When he described how the Shark had tried to kill him, then how Meier had kidnapped him and taken him to the 'safe house', it was really too horrible. But eventually Hiro came to the end, and looked up at Fischer helplessly. This man was his last hope!

Fischer watched Hiro for a moment or two, then nodded. 'Well, that's quite a story, Mr Adachi, quite a story indeed. Right, let's see if we can sort this out.' He paused and looked at Hiro seriously. 'What was the name of the old man on the train?'

'Erik Björnson, I think,' Hiro said.

'Very good.' Fischer gave another nod. Immediately he reached across to the phone and pressed one of the buttons. A quick conversation in German followed. Hiro understood nothing except the name Erik Björnson. At last the conversation came to an end. Fischer put down the phone, then calmly put his hands together as before.

'Well, good news, Mr Adachi. First of all, I'm happy to tell you that there's no one by the name of Erik Björnson staying in the hotel – not in Room 319, nor in any other. And the guest in Room 319 is someone called Schmidt. Mr Schmidt is a regular customer, I'm told. Does this information make you feel any less worried?'

Hiro remained silent. Being Japanese, he always felt it was polite to agree. But this time he simply couldn't do it. He moved uncomfortably in his seat.

'You still don't look happy, Mr Adachi,' Fischer continued.

Hiro didn't know what to say. He searched for words. 'But the Shark may be using another name,' he said at last. 'He may not even be staying at the hotel. Don't you see, he could walk in at any time?' Hiro began to feel helpless again. Surely Fischer could understand what he was saying? Why did everyone think he was just a crazy student from Japan?

Fischer looked at Hiro a little impatiently. 'I'm sorry, Mr Adachi, but I think we've done as much as possible. For anything further, I really think you must return to the police.'

'But in half an hour it'll be eight o'clock!' Hiro cried.

'Then perhaps you shouldn't waste any more time discussing it with me,' Fischer replied sharply.

Hiro didn't know what to do. His last chance was running away like sand through his fingers.

'I must ask you to leave now, Mr Adachi. We've done all we can,' Fischer said. He got to his feet. 'I'd like to thank you for your trouble. My colleague will show you out of the hotel. Hans!' Fischer said a few words in German to the man in uniform at the door. Hiro had forgotten the man was there.

Hiro knew it was useless to say any more.

The man in uniform moved forward. 'Please follow me,' he said.

Hiro didn't argue. He followed the man through the corridors with his head down. He felt terribly tired.

They came out into the reception area. The bright lights hurt Hiro's eyes. The man led the way across towards the revolving door. Hiro's mind was completely empty; he had given all he could.

The man stopped at the door. '*Sayonara*,' he said in Japanese, with an unpleasant smile.

Hiro gave a shake of his head, but was too tired to say goodbye himself. He looked up at the door. It was already turning: an old man was just coming in, pulling a small case on wheels behind him. From his hat and clothes Hiro guessed the man must be a priest. Hiro stepped into the doorway and began moving through. At that moment the priest's eyes met Hiro's. They stared at him for one second only, then looked away, but there was something about the stare that Hiro recognised.

The next moment, as he stood on the pavement outside, Hiro realised who had just entered the hotel. It was the Shark.

Chapter 14 *Inside the Hotel Adlon*

For a second or two Hiro was completely unable to move. Even though the old man looked quite different dressed as a priest, Hiro was absolutely certain who it was. But the idea that the Shark might change his appearance had never really entered Hiro's head before. The memory of the priest he'd seen at the Brandenburg Gate came back to him – of course, that was the Shark!

He was sure too that the Shark had recognised him. Hiro's legs were shaking, but he couldn't stop staring in through the hotel window. The Shark was at the reception desk and was talking to the receptionist. The two of them seemed to be looking back at the door. Hiro turned away and walked quickly up the road.

What should he do? His first thought was to turn and go back into the hotel, but he stopped himself immediately. As well as being a stupid and dangerous thing to do, Hiro knew he wouldn't get past the door. One of the men in uniform was sure to stop him at the entrance. Hiro knew as well that there was no point going back to the police – even if they listened to him, it would be too late. With a sick feeling in his stomach, he realised that if he were going to do anything, he would have to do it by himself.

Hiro walked up and down the street. 'Think!' he kept saying to himself. 'Come on! You must think!' The sick feeling got worse with every second that passed. The Shark was in the hotel. Hiro had to act fast!

He reached the end of the building, then stopped. A crazy idea came to him then.

There was no time to lose. Guessing that the hotel must have an underground car park, Hiro hurried back past the hotel entrance, then turned down the next side road. Thirty metres later, he found what he was looking for. A metal bar stretched across the entrance of the car park and there was an office to one side. Hiro walked past a couple of times, looking in at the office. A man was sitting at the window, with three or four TV screens above him, but he was more interested in the newspaper open on his desk.

After making sure there was no one watching, Hiro hurried beneath the office window, then round the metal bar. It was simple. He was in!

On one side of the car park he saw a row of expensive cars; on the other a sign read '*Ablieferungen*'. Hiro had no idea what it meant, but a few moments later a large white van with pictures of fruit and vegetables on the side arrived. Hiro guessed he must be near the hotel kitchens and that the sign he had seen meant 'Deliveries'.

There were voices just up ahead. Hiro dropped down behind a car and looked carefully round the next corner. A couple of young men were standing outside a doorway, smoking. They were wearing the white jackets of kitchen workers and they looked a little guilty, as if they were breaking some kind of rule. Hiro just waited and watched.

After five minutes, still laughing and chatting, they went back inside. Hiro waited half a minute longer, then ran up to the doorway where the two men had disappeared. The door was still half open. He pushed his way inside and found himself in a narrow corridor.

Up ahead he could hear the sounds of the kitchen. He moved forward. Halfway down the corridor there was a door on the left. He stopped and listened. No sound. Very carefully he opened the door and looked inside.

On one wall there was just a long shelf with huge cans of food, but when he looked on the other side of the room, he couldn't believe his luck. On the back of another door, Hiro saw three or four white jackets, similar to the ones the smokers had been wearing. If he put on one of these, Hiro thought, he might be able to get through the kitchens without being stopped.

There was no time for further thought. Hiro tried on the first jacket. It was far too big. He put it back and took the next. This time it was fine. He quickly buttoned the jacket all the way up to the neck and headed straight to the door.

Then he stopped. Perhaps it would be better if he was carrying something; it was less likely that he'd be stopped. Turning back, he picked up two of the big cans of food, then decided to take a third can too, as it would hide half of his face. Then he went out through the door.

He walked quickly. He couldn't stop and look around. He had to appear to know where he was going. He had to just trust his luck.

To his amazement, it went like a dream. Hiro walked straight down the corridor and a couple of seconds later found himself inside a huge kitchen. There were three men over to the right standing near the ovens, but they didn't even look up, each busy at his job.

Hiro walked straight ahead, then reached a half-open door. As he did so, he heard someone coming in the other direction. Immediately, Hiro turned round and pushed his way through the door with his back – because he was carrying something it was the most natural thing to do. The other man hurried past without saying a word.

Once he was through the door, Hiro found himself in a hall. There were further doors to the right and left. Long corridors led away almost out of view. In front of him there were stairs and the doors of a lift.

Hiro thought about the lift. If it was a service lift, used only by hotel workers, it might go all the way to the top of the building. He took a deep breath and pressed the button. The lift doors opened immediately. He stepped inside, then came out again. The cans he'd been carrying had been useful, but now he needed something else.

Hiro put the cans down under the staircase, then noticed a pile of dirty sheets there. If he was carrying sheets, Hiro hoped he would again be mistaken for one of the hotel workers. He picked the sheets up and entered the lift just as the doors closed. He looked round for the buttons. Yes, it was just as he'd guessed! There were two floors below ground level, and seven above. If only his luck could continue. Surely, it was logical for Room 319 to be on the third floor!

He pressed the button showing '3'. The lift began to travel up.

Chapter 15   *A little bit of Schubert*

When the lift came to a stop, Hiro stepped out to find himself in a small area used only by hotel workers. Opposite the lift, there was a door. Hiro pushed it open. The next moment, as if going through a secret entrance hidden in the wall, he came out into a public corridor of the hotel. He was halfway along. The corridor, its floor covered in deep red carpet, stretched in both directions.

Hiro didn't know which way to go. He chose one way, but saw that the numbers on the doors were going up: 325, 327, 329. So he turned round, and the numbers on the doors began to go down, even numbers on the left, odd numbers on the right. He followed them down: 325, 323, 321. As he passed this last room, he felt his heart begin to beat very fast.

All of a sudden he was there: Room 319. He was about to knock, when he stopped himself. He realised he had no idea what he was going to say or do. His confidence suddenly left him. Was he really so certain a murder was about to take place?

Hiro didn't hear the door to the room behind him open. Out of nowhere, he heard a voice speaking in German.

Hiro turned to see a man of about thirty standing in the doorway of Room 320. The man looked quite tough – like a soldier perhaps, but in ordinary clothes.

Hiro felt helpless. 'I'm sorry, I don't understand German,' he said in English.

The man looked confused. 'You don't speak German?'

'No,' Hiro said.

The man narrowed his eyes. 'But you work here?'

Hiro felt weak at the knees. He'd forgotten the white jacket and the sheets he was carrying; now he couldn't think how to explain them. 'No, I'm a student,' he said quietly. 'But I must see the man in this room, Mr Schmidt. I have some important information for him.'

Immediately the man's body became tight. 'I think you'd better tell me first. I'm a colleague of Mr Schmidt.'

Hiro didn't know what to say.

'Well, I'm waiting,' the man went on.

Hiro wasn't sure if he could trust the man. But there was no time to decide. Hiro had to give an explanation. 'I came to see Mr Schmidt because …' he began, then stopped. 'Well, his life might be in danger.'

Now the man's eyes became very sharp. 'We'd better talk about this in my room,' he said after a moment. His voice made it clear that Hiro shouldn't argue.

The man stood back and let Hiro go past into the room. As soon as they were both inside, the man shut the door quickly and looked through the eyehole to the corridor outside.

'Please sit down,' the man said, turning back to Hiro.

Hiro dropped the sheets behind the door and chose the nearest chair.

The man continued immediately. 'OK, you say you're a student?' He didn't sit down or wait for an answer. 'So, what information do you have for Mr Schmidt?'

'I was on the train to Berlin,' Hiro began, his voice shaking. 'By accident I looked at another man's phone and read a message – two messages, in fact. They talked about an assignment here in this hotel in Room 319 this evening.'

The man looked surprised. 'Go on,' he said quickly.

'Well, the man on the train. He tried to kill me. And he's in the hotel now. I saw him only twenty minutes ago.'

At that, the man pulled up another chair and sat very close. His voice became very serious. 'This isn't a student joke, is it?' he said. 'It's very important. Do you understand?'

'Yes, I do.' Hiro looked straight back into the man's eyes. 'I was kidnapped as well,' he added after a moment. 'I've been very frightened.'

The man paused, then nodded. 'Do you know who Mr Schmidt really is?'

Hiro shook his head. 'No. What do you mean? Isn't Schmidt his real name?'

'No, it isn't.' The man watched Hiro closely. After a moment's thought, he went on: 'Listen, I'm going to tell you things which perhaps I shouldn't. But it seems there's very little time, so I'll have to take a chance. It doesn't matter who Schmidt is – it's enough to know he's someone extremely important. And for reasons I can't explain, Mr Schmidt is here in the hotel secretly.'

'OK,' Hiro answered.

'Well, I'm his bodyguard – his personal bodyguard – I'm here to make sure he's safe. Normally he has several bodyguards with him, but as he's here in secret I'm the only one with him tonight. Understand?'

Hiro nodded.

The man was very serious now, sitting forward closely. 'Now who is this man who's come to kill him? What does he look like?'

Hiro coughed. For a second he couldn't speak. 'He's old … but there's something really frightening about him. He's like a shark – he's got the same eyes and teeth. On the train he said his name was Erik Björnson and that he was a businessman, but he came into the hotel this evening dressed as a priest.'

'A priest!' the man repeated.

'Yes, I'm sure of it,' replied Hiro.

The man jumped up from his chair and went to the door. For a moment he looked through the eyehole. Then he stood back. He thought for a second or two, then spoke again. 'OK, listen. There's no time to call my colleagues, so I'm going to need your help. What's your phone number?'

Hiro felt very frightened now, but he also had the wonderful feeling that he wasn't on his own any more – someone had believed him at last. He told the man his number and the man typed it into his own phone. Immediately, he pressed 'Call'. Hiro's phone began to ring, then stopped.

'Right,' the man said, 'you've got my number now as well.' He paused and sat down opposite Hiro again. 'OK, this is what I want you to do. I'm going to try and get the pr—, I mean, Mr Schmidt, out of this place, or at least into another room. I want you to stay here. Stand by the door and look out through the eyehole. If this guy shows up – the priest, that is – the second you see him, call my number. Is that clear?'

'Yes,' Hiro answered.

'Good.' The man sat up. He looked at Hiro for a second, then said, 'What's your name?'

'Hiro Adachi.'

'Mine's Schubert, Franz Schubert,' the man replied. He immediately held up his hand. 'Yes, I know, there's a famous composer with the same name. My parents were crazy about classical music. Anyway, please call me Franz.'

'OK, Franz,' Hiro said.

'Great,' Schubert answered. He put a hand on Hiro's shoulder. 'You've done brilliantly, Hiro. And you've been very brave.'

He didn't delay any longer. Giving Hiro a nod, he got to his feet, picked up a small bag by the wall and went to the door. 'OK, this is it,' he said. As he did so, he reached inside his jacket and pulled out a gun. There was something very cold-looking about the black metal. Then he dropped his arm down by his side. 'See you in fifteen minutes,' he said in a whisper.

The next moment the man had gone. Silence fell inside the room.

Hiro looked at the door. Fear suddenly filled him. He was on his own again.

Chapter 16   *A visit from the priest*

Hiro stood there staring at the door for five or six seconds, then suddenly remembered he had a job to do. Without wasting another moment, he looked through the eyehole.

The view was better than he expected. He could see a couple of metres down the corridor in addition to the door of Room 319 opposite. Schubert was there at that moment. Hiro could see him looking up and down the corridor, the gun still down at his side.

About ten seconds later, the door to Room 319 opened. A woman, blonde and very attractive, wearing a red nightdress, stood in the doorway. She and Schubert talked for a moment, then she stepped back with a worried look on her face. Schubert went inside with her and the door closed immediately.

A minute passed. Hiro kept his eye to the door, only checking that Schubert's number was shown under 'Last Call' on his phone.

When he looked back someone had come into view in the corridor outside. Hiro's heart beat faster. Could it be the Shark? Hiro looked more closely. No, it was a boy of sixteen or seventeen, wearing a smart hotel uniform. In his hand he was carrying a message on a metal plate. But could it be one of the Shark's friends? Hiro watched through the eyehole as the boy came directly to Hiro's door and knocked.

Hiro didn't know what to do. He didn't want to open the door, but perhaps it really was a hotel worker. Perhaps the message was important – something Schubert should know. Hiro saw the boy look down the corridor, then heard him knock again, harder.

This time Hiro decided he must answer. Very carefully, he opened the door. It was only half-open when there was a dull sound twice: *dumf! dumf!* one after another. At the same moment the boy seemed to throw himself on Hiro, his arms flying round him almost like a lover. Hiro was knocked back, crashed against the wall, and fell to the floor. The boy came down on top of him and lay there without moving. The plate he'd been holding banged loudly against the door.

Hiro tried to get to his feet. He was so confused that for three or four seconds he still didn't understand that the boy had been shot. Then someone else appeared in the doorway. It was the Shark. He was still dressed as a priest, but he was now holding a silenced gun at his side. Hiro tried to speak, but no sound would come from his mouth.

'Yes, my friend, it's me,' said the Shark, with a sickly smile. 'I apologise for my violent entry.' He kicked the legs of the young hotel worker out of the way and closed the door immediately. 'A most unlucky young man. I needed some way to make you open the door,' he went on, 'and unfortunately for this boy, I chose him.' Then, getting down so he was level with Hiro, he continued, 'Right, now listen, my Japanese friend. I have very little time. I saw you come into this room and now I need some information.'

Still fighting to get his breath, Hiro managed to pull himself free from the body on top of him. As he did so, Hiro saw his jeans were covered in blood. For a second he thought he was bleeding, then he realised the blood belonged to the hotel worker. A scream grew in Hiro's throat, but wouldn't come out.

The Shark had his face close to Hiro's. His teeth seemed very bright. 'In a short time I am going to kill you.'

Hiro was completely unable to speak.

The Shark nodded his head. 'Yes, be sure of this – I will kill you. But I can do it in two ways.' He came even closer. 'The first way is with a bullet in the middle of the head. Like this …' He pressed the gun into the middle of Hiro's forehead and made a clicking sound with his tongue, then pulled it away. 'You will not feel a thing. Very clean, very quick – you will like it!' He paused. 'Or I can shoot you in the stomach. The pain is terrible, please believe me.' His eyes seemed to dance with pleasure as he considered this. 'Yes, very terrible. That is why you Japanese commit *hara-kiri* by tearing a knife through the stomach – because death is so slow and you suffer so much. Very brave people, you Japanese.'

Now the Shark sat back on his heels, and watched Hiro thoughtfully. 'So that is your choice, my friend. If you tell me what I wish to know, *pop, pop* in the head, all very fast. If you don't, you will die very slowly. So, which will you choose?'

All the time the Shark was speaking, Hiro was trying to think what he could do. Was there nothing? Was this really the end? All day long he had been putting himself in danger, but somehow it hadn't seemed real. It had felt almost like a computer game which he could turn off when he'd had enough. Now this was completely real. He wanted to complain that the rules hadn't been properly explained, but he knew it was useless. He thought of Akiko suddenly. Would he never see her again after all?

'So, which is it to be?' The Shark pressed the gun hard into Hiro's stomach and smiled.

Hiro didn't answer. Thinking of Akiko had suddenly given him an idea. His phone was still in his hand. Could he manage to call Schubert without looking at the keys? He knew his phone so well – where all the different keys were and what they all did. If he could just get his hand in his pocket so it was out of view. All he needed to do then was bring up Schubert's number and press the 'Call' key.

The Shark was waiting for his answer. 'Well?'

'What do you want to know?' Hiro said quickly.

The Shark seemed surprised. 'So, you choose the head! This is very good. Right, I need to know this.'

Hiro had managed to sit up against the wall, and already he had his hand with his phone in it in his pocket. He turned the phone around in his hand. Was it the correct way up? He had to feel for the keys, but without pressing too hard!

'The man who went into Room 319,' the Shark began. 'He is a bodyguard, yes?'

'Yes,' Hiro answered. He had the phone the correct way up. He was sure of it. OK, now to bring up Schubert's number he had to press the 'Back' key.

'And he is the only bodyguard, yes?'

'Yes,' Hiro replied. His fingers felt around the keypad. Top right. That was the one to press. He did so without delay.

'And why has the bodyguard gone into the room?'

Hiro paused. 'He's going to move Schmidt to another room, I think.'

The Shark gave a short laugh. 'Schmidt! Ha! That's very good. And has the bodyguard called for any help?'

Hiro didn't answer. He was trying to think about the phone. The 'Call' key – it was top left, wasn't it? Or was it? Suddenly he wasn't so certain.

'Come on!' The Shark's eyes were full of sudden anger. 'Answer me! Are there more men coming? Do they know my description?'

'No!' Hiro answered. 'I don't know, I don't think so.'

'You are lying! You told him I was dressed as a priest, didn't you?'

Just as he was about to answer, Hiro remembered: the 'Call' key wasn't at the top, it was the one below it.

'Well?' the Shark shouted.

'Maybe,' Hiro said quietly.

'Ah, the truth at last!' The Shark sat back for a moment, looking pleased. 'Anyway, it does not matter, I have what I need.' He sat forward again. 'My friend, the time has come. I am sorry that it is not possible to get to know you better – you seem a very brave young man. But …' The Shark lifted his hands as if in apology.

Hiro felt a tight ball of fear rise in his throat again. His fingers moved over the keys on his phone again. Was this right? Did he have the correct key? There was no time to think about it any more. He pressed hard with his thumb.

The Shark raised the gun and pointed it at Hiro's head.

Hiro thought he might cry. He had to keep the Shark talking. How long would it be before Schubert replied? Schubert was Hiro's last hope.

Wait!' Hiro called hopelessly. 'Please, please, I know you're going to kill me, but will you do one thing for me?'

The old man suddenly gave a grandfatherly look. 'A dying wish?' His eyes went small again. 'What is it?'

Hiro had to keep the Shark talking for just a few seconds more. He said the first thing that came into his head. 'It's my girlfriend, Akiko. We broke up just before I came to Berlin. Will you send her a message for me?'

'Ha!' The Shark gave a sudden laugh. 'How romantic! Now I am to bring two lovers together in death!'

Hiro was unable to breathe. Perhaps he'd got the keys all wrong. Maybe there wasn't any hope …

'And what is the tearful message you wish me to send?' The Shark had his caring look again.

'Please tell her …' Hiro started.

'Yes?' said the Shark.

'I want you to tell her …' Hiro began again.

The Shark suddenly tired of the game. 'Bah! You are trying to waste time. You think I am stupid?'

'No!' cried Hiro. All of a sudden there was a tiny sound. It came from Hiro's pocket.

There was silence in the room for a second.

Then it came again. It was a voice. 'Hiro?' it said quietly. Then more loudly, 'Hiro, it's Franz!'

Chapter 17 *A surprise visitor*

'What is that?' the Shark asked sharply.

'I don't know,' Hiro lied. He could hear Schubert saying his name repeatedly.

'It is your phone!' the Shark said. His eyes were on fire. 'Give it to me!'

Very slowly, Hiro took the phone from his pocket.

Schubert's voice was clear all of a sudden. 'Hiro? Hiro? What's going on?' Hiro could hardly believe it. The plan had worked!

But now the Shark was boiling with anger. He shouted a word in a foreign language that Hiro didn't recognise, then went back to English. 'What have you done? You have called this man!' He was shaking the gun right in front of Hiro's eyes. The Shark's face suddenly became very hard.

This is it, Hiro thought. Now comes the shot. Schubert had stopped speaking now. Perhaps he was crossing the corridor at that moment; perhaps he would crash through the door any second. But it didn't matter what the bodyguard did now. Hiro knew it would be too late. Helplessly, he put his hand up in front of his face as if he imagined he could stop the bullets. He prepared himself for the shot.

But it didn't come. Instead, the Shark pulled the phone from Hiro's hand.

'Who is this?' the Shark said angrily into the phone.

Hiro couldn't hear what Schubert replied. The gun was still pointing at Hiro's head and it was very difficult to think.

'Right,' the Shark went on in a new quieter voice. 'Listen to me. I believe you know who you are talking to. As you must know, I have the Japanese boy with me. If you try anything stupid, I will shoot him immediately. Is that clear?'

Again Hiro supposed that Schubert replied, but he had no idea what Schubert said. The Shark interrupted.

'All right, shut up! Listen to me. I am going to leave this hotel with the boy and you will not do anything to stop me. I have already killed one of the hotel workers. Now, this is what I want. Are you listening carefully?' He got quickly to his feet, made his way over to the door, and looked through the eyehole. Next he went over to the window, and looked out into the night. All the time he kept the gun pointing at Hiro. Very soon he came back.

'In a couple of minutes' time, the boy and I are going to leave this room. We will go down to the back entrance of the hotel – I want you to have a taxi waiting there for us. I will tell the driver where to go, but you will not attempt to follow the taxi. If there is trouble at any point, the Japanese boy will die. Is that clear? I will give you three minutes to arrange this. Call me back when everything is ready.'

The Shark pressed the 'End Call' key and dropped the phone into his pocket. Then he looked across to Hiro. 'This does not mean you will live after all,' he said. 'If I could, I would kill you twice!'

Listening to the Shark, Hiro felt strangely dead already. He was so tired; the last twenty-four hours had been so hard. It seemed as if he was watching himself in a crazy film, watching helplessly as it showed the story of his life.

'Get up!' the Shark said, coming towards him with the gun again.

Hiro climbed slowly to his feet. He wondered what was coming next.

'Now, go over to the door and pull the boy out of the way,' the Shark ordered.

Hiro felt ill again. He moved across and reached down for the boy's arms. It didn't hit him till then that the boy was really dead. Other than his grandfather, this was the first time Hiro had seen a dead person. When he tried to lift the boy's shoulders they felt so heavy and so warm. Was there really no life? Only ten minutes before, the boy had been knocking cheerfully on the door. Hiro wanted to cry.

The Shark was watching him closely. 'First time?' he asked coldly. 'Have no fear. Dead people don't usually complain.' He gave his horrible toothy smile for a moment, then his face went hard again. 'Come on – don't waste time.'

Hiro pulled at the body in his arms. 'I'm sorry,' he said under his breath. At last the body moved. As Hiro pulled the boy across the carpet a long bright red line of blood was left behind. Hiro thought he would be sick.

A moment later Hiro's phone rang again in the Shark's pocket. Hiro saw the Shark reach into his clothes, then a number of things happened very suddenly. First of all there was a very bright light and a terrific explosion, then the room went completely dark. At the same time a cloud of smoke filled the room. Hiro heard shots: again the *dumf! dumf!* of a silenced gun – then a loud cry of 'Aaghh!' followed by the crashing of furniture. After that there was a strange silence, like the end of the world. For a moment or two Hiro wondered if he was dead.

Then the lights came on again.

It took a little while for the smoke in the room to clear. When it did, Hiro saw that the door to the room had gone. It lay on the floor, broken in pieces. Standing over it was Schubert. On the floor opposite him lay the Shark. The old man was still alive, but he was holding his stomach very tightly. Already blood had started to appear through the priest's clothes; no matter how hard he held his stomach, he couldn't seem to stop it.

'Sorry to come in without knocking,' Schubert said coolly.

The Shark's eyes were tight with pain. Very slowly, he turned his head and looked directly at Hiro. His face had gone as white as a sheet, but his teeth still shone in the bright light.

In a quiet voice he said, 'I wish I had chosen another seat on the train.'

Chapter 18 *A note of thanks*

At two o'clock the next afternoon Hiro was sitting with Schubert in the Funkturm Restaurant, halfway up the famous TV and radio tower in the Spandau area of Berlin. It was a beautiful day. The sun was shining and from up there, you could see far across the city – huge roads busy with traffic, parks, even lakes and forests far away outside the city. In the distance a jet was just climbing into the air from the airport; it seemed to stick in the sky without moving.

'This restaurant is famous for its seafood,' Schubert said, looking at the menu. 'Why don't we go for that?'

'It's very expensive,' Hiro answered, noticing the prices.

'Don't worry about that,' Schubert said quickly. 'Someone very rich is paying. Let's make the most of it!'

Without discussing it any more, Schubert gave the waiter their order. When the waiter had gone, Schubert turned to the window. 'There. Berlin's not so bad, is it?' he said, pointing at the view.

Hiro was about to answer when Schubert's mobile phone rang. Schubert listened quietly to a message for half a minute or so, then excused himself and went off to a quiet part of the restaurant in order to continue the conversation.

While Schubert was gone, Hiro thought back over what had happened that morning. They had spent most of the time in Schubert's head office. 'The *Bundesamt für Verfassungsschutz* – Home Security,' Schubert had said by way of explanation. There, Hiro had spent two hours in front of a computer screen looking at photos of known criminals. The only man Hiro could definitely recognise was the driver who had picked him up with Meier. Hiro was disappointed, but Schubert wasn't. Once they found this man, he said darkly, it would be simple to get Meier and anyone else.

After that Schubert had said it was time for lunch. Schubert had put a blue emergency light on the roof of his BMW and they'd raced through the streets of Berlin, laughing like a pair of silly children. The journey had made Hiro feel happier than he had been for weeks – and very important.

Now, sitting up there in the restaurant, drink in hand, Hiro found it hard to believe all the things that had happened. He felt so safe and relaxed now, looking out across the city. Had the Shark really tried to kill him? It seemed like a dream. Had it all really happened?

As if in answer to Hiro's thoughts, Schubert came back to the table and sat down. He looked at Hiro before speaking.

'He's dead,' he said.

Hiro was confused for a moment.

'Our friend, the Shark. He died an hour ago.'

'Oh,' Hiro said. It felt as if a cold hand had run down his back. 'I'm sorry,' he said.

'Don't be sorry,' Schubert replied quickly. 'The man was a professional assassin. He made his living from death. He nearly killed you too.'

'Yes, I know,' Hiro answered.

'Anyway, let's give him his real name. I've just been told he was actually a Norwegian by the name of Karl-Henrik Johansen. Interpol, the International Police, have apparently been looking for him for years. He was wanted for eleven murders – one of them the president of a certain country in South America.'

Hiro didn't know what to say. He kept remembering the last time he had seen the Shark, as the old man was being carried to the ambulance, his face white with pain.

'Of course, it was because he came from abroad that he needed to collect a gun from Meier at the Brandenburg Gate. It would be much too dangerous to try and bring a gun into the country.'

Hiro went silent. Every mention now of the gun reminded Hiro of the young hotel worker.

Schubert was watching Hiro carefully. 'What's wrong?' he asked quietly. 'Is it the boy?'

Hiro nodded. 'I keep remembering …'

Schubert reached out an arm. 'Try not to think about that.' Very gently, he added, 'If it helps at all, I can tell you he didn't suffer – he was killed immediately – the shots went through his heart.'

Neither man spoke for a while.

Hiro tried to think about something else. When he felt calmer again he said, 'I'm surprised the Shark decided to continue with the assassination plan after what happened.'

'Yes, it was a bad mistake.' Schubert looked at Hiro. 'I think he didn't like losing to a kid …' Schubert seemed embarrassed for a moment, then went on quickly, 'I'm sorry. I'm not suggesting you're a kid – but I guess the Shark thought of you like that. You were brilliant, you know,' Schubert added. 'What you did was very, very special.'

Now it was Hiro's turn to be embarrassed. Fortunately, at that moment the waiter arrived, so Hiro didn't need to answer. A huge plate of seafood was placed in front of him – Hiro suddenly realised he was terrifically hungry.

'*Guten Appetit*,' Schubert said.

'*Itadakimasu*,' Hiro replied.

They both ate happily in silence for a short time. Then Schubert sat back and looked closely at Hiro.

'Hiro, I need to talk to you about Mr Schmidt,' he began. 'You've been so extraordinarily brave it's only fair you should know something about him. But I'm very sorry, I still can't tell you his real name. I will say this though: the person whose life you saved is very, very important.'

'He's in the government?' Hiro asked.

Schubert looked directly at Hiro. 'I can't say. But he's someone of the very highest importance.'

'And you can't tell me why the Shark was hired to kill him either, I suppose …' Hiro said.

Schubert gave a weak smile. 'Important people make important enemies. We think Meier's men have been trying to kill Schmidt for months. After an earlier plan failed, it seems they decided to hire the best – that is, the Shark.'

Hiro was confused. 'Then why … why was Schmidt in a hotel with only you there – why was he there in secret?'

Schubert looked embarrassed again. After a moment he sat forward. 'Sometimes, Hiro, a man like Mr Schmidt has part of his life he wishes to keep private. That's why he meets his friend in a hotel. That's why I was the only bodyguard at the hotel. Do you understand what I'm saying?'

Hiro suddenly remembered the blonde woman who had opened the door of Schmidt's hotel room. 'You mean …' he said slowly.

'Somehow Meier and his men found out about Mr Schmidt's …' Schubert searched for the right word. 'Mr Schmidt's arrangement. When they did, they saw an opportunity to kill him.'

Hiro stared at Schubert. The man had told him as much as he could. Hiro nodded. 'I think I understand. Thank you for telling me.'

Schubert shook his head. 'No, no, we must thank you.' He gave a little cough. 'Actually, while we're on that subject, I have something for you.' He reached into his pocket, pulled out an envelope and held it for a moment.

'Mr Schmidt asked me to give you this,' Schubert said and handed the envelope across.

Hiro looked at it for a moment or two.

'Go on, open it,' Schubert said.

Hiro did as he was told. Inside there was a second envelope and a small hand-written note. In English, the note read:

'Thank you so much for all you have done for me. You are a true *samurai*. Enjoy your trip.'

The note was signed with the single word: 'Schmidt'.

Hiro put down the note and opened the second envelope. Inside were ten completely new five-hundred-euro notes.

Chapter 19   *A friendly word of advice*

Two hours later, after a delicious lunch, Hiro and Schubert took the lift back down to the ground. They climbed into Schubert's BMW and set off back to the city centre. Schubert wasn't in any hurry and this time he drove much more slowly, window down, enjoying the sunshine.

After the excitement of the meal and the money from Schmidt, Hiro suddenly felt strangely empty. He had the odd feeling that he was returning to real life at last. In one way that was good: to know that he was safe was wonderful. But returning to reality also meant remembering his break-up with Akiko. How he wished he could share Schmidt's present with her!

It was as if Schubert could read his thoughts. The very next moment, looking across as he drove, Schubert asked, 'So, my friend, have you decided how to spend the money?'

Hiro bit his lip. He looked away, out of the window. 'I'm not sure,' he said quietly. 'I think I might save it.'

'What?' Schubert cried out. 'Come on! Don't be so boring. Enjoy part of it, at least. Fly somewhere! Go somewhere special! Take your girlfriend!'

It was the very worst thing Schubert could say. For a moment Hiro thought he might break into tears – the last twenty-four hours had taken all his strength. He bit his lip so hard this time, that he tasted blood.

Schubert noticed. 'Hey, did I say something wrong?' he asked more gently.

Hiro felt too tired to lie. 'I broke up with my girlfriend just before I came here,' he said at last.

Schubert looked embarrassed. 'I'm sorry.' Very quietly, he added, 'And it was her decision, not yours?'

Hiro nodded. 'I still don't know how it happened. I thought we were really happy together.' He closed his eyes as all the memories came back.

A hundred metres up the road Schubert stopped the car. 'Why don't you tell me about it?' he said. 'What happened?'

Hiro opened his eyes. They were next to a park. In the distance he could see a young couple walking hand-in-hand through the trees.

'I just don't understand,' Hiro began. He shook his head again. 'We had a terrible argument. We were planning a holiday together. Then, out of nowhere, this awful fight started.'

'Go on,' Schubert said.

'Well, this is going to sound crazy, but it was about my dog. I have a dog, Yuki – she's a golden retriever. Anyway, I have her photo on my phone as the screensaver. My girlfriend thought her photo should be there instead. I couldn't understand how she could be jealous of a dog.'

Schubert made an odd face. 'Really? It doesn't sound like a good reason to break up. Are you sure there wasn't something else?'

Hiro looked back at Schubert. 'What do you mean?'

'Well, people don't always talk about things directly, Hiro. Come on, you know that. Girls are the worst! There was probably another reason.'

Hiro tried to think back. He could remember the whole argument perfectly. He'd come to her room to talk, to tell her that he'd asked Daijiro and Ayumu and their girlfriends to join the trip. And Akiko had been fine with that. She'd said, 'Great, that's lovely.' She'd said, 'The more, the better!' She didn't seem to mind … She didn't …

Schubert broke into Hiro's thoughts. 'What is it?'

'I've just thought of something. When we were planning our trip, I thought it would be nice if we invited some others. You don't think …?'

'Go on,' said Schubert.

'Well, it was a couple of guys and their girlfriends. You don't think she was jealous about that, do you?' Hiro asked. Just as he said it, a horrible idea came crashing into his head. Ayumu's girlfriend was Risa. Risa was from Hiro's college in Japan and he'd once invited her out. Perhaps Akiko had found out about that. Perhaps she thought …

Schubert looked at Hiro and shook his head. 'Oh dear, my friend,' he said. 'You may be too clever for an international assassin, but it seems a young woman is too much for you. You were planning a romantic holiday for two, and then you invite another two girls along. I imagine the girls are pretty?'

Hiro felt suddenly very sick. 'So-so,' he answered, giving a small cough.

'Well, of course, she was jealous!' Schubert broke in. 'She simply pretended it was the dog, so she didn't have to admit it was the girls. What happened afterwards?'

'She said she never wanted to see me again,' Hiro replied.

'So, you believed her, I suppose. And being a brave *samurai,* you've been too proud to call her again. I guess you didn't apologise?' asked Schubert.

Hiro didn't say anything. He felt a mix of anger and sudden love for Schubert. The man had made him feel terribly stupid and small.

Schubert watched Hiro. For about ten seconds neither of them said anything. Then Schubert spoke again:

'Right, my friend, you've done something for me. Now I'm going to do something for you. Get out your phone.'

Hiro didn't argue.

'Now find me her number,' Schubert ordered.

Hiro's heart had begun to beat very hard. He selected 'Menu', then 'Phone book', then found Akiko's number.

'OK.' Schubert got out of the car. He walked round to the passenger door, opened it, then said very strongly, 'Right. Get out.' Hiro did as he was told.

Schubert pointed across the park. 'Do you see that seat over there? You're going to walk over to it and sit down. And then you're going to press that number.'

Hiro realised his lip was shaking. 'What shall I say?'

'You'll think of something,' Schubert replied.

Hiro didn't move for a moment or two. Then he felt Schubert's hand on his back, pushing him away.

Hiro walked slowly up the path. His legs felt heavy, almost too heavy to move. The sun was hot on the back of his neck as well and he felt a little sick from all the food. At last he reached the seat and sat down.

He looked across at the car. Schubert was sitting inside again, watching through the window. Hiro felt nearly as nervous as when the Shark had pointed the gun at his head. He looked at the phone and the photo of Akiko. Then he took a deep breath.

A couple of seconds later, he pressed 'Call'.